TRUCKS GALORE

Peter Stein
illustrated by Bob Staake

Candlewick Press

Wide truck, thin truck,
out truck, in truck.
Hot truck, cold truck,
big bad BOLD truck!

Strong truck, weak truck,
hide-and-seek truck.
Rock truck, dirt truck,
Yum — DESSERT truck!

Trucks and MORE trucks!
Open-door trucks!
Heavy-load trucks!
Shake-the-road trucks!

Baaa truck. Moo truck.
Cock-a-doodle-DOO truck.
Oink truck. Cluck truck.
Quackin' in a duck truck!

STOP

Trucks on job sites,
working hard.
Trucks protecting,
standing guard.

Hey, you trucks!
CLEAN UP THAT YARD!

USA

Outer-space truck.
Out-of-place truck.
Song-and-dance truck.
Lost-his-pants truck!

Burning building!
Screeching tires!
Water gushing!
Trucks for FIRES!

Bird truck, weird truck,
bushy-beard truck.
Round truck, bent truck,
circus-tent truck!

Trucks and trucks and
even MORE trucks!
Loaded roads of
trucks GALORE trucks!

HOT DOG TOWN

Stranded auto,
stuck in muck.
Not for long . . .
TOW IT, TRUCK!

Stinky GARBAGE . . .
outta here!
Trucks can make it
DISAPPEAR!

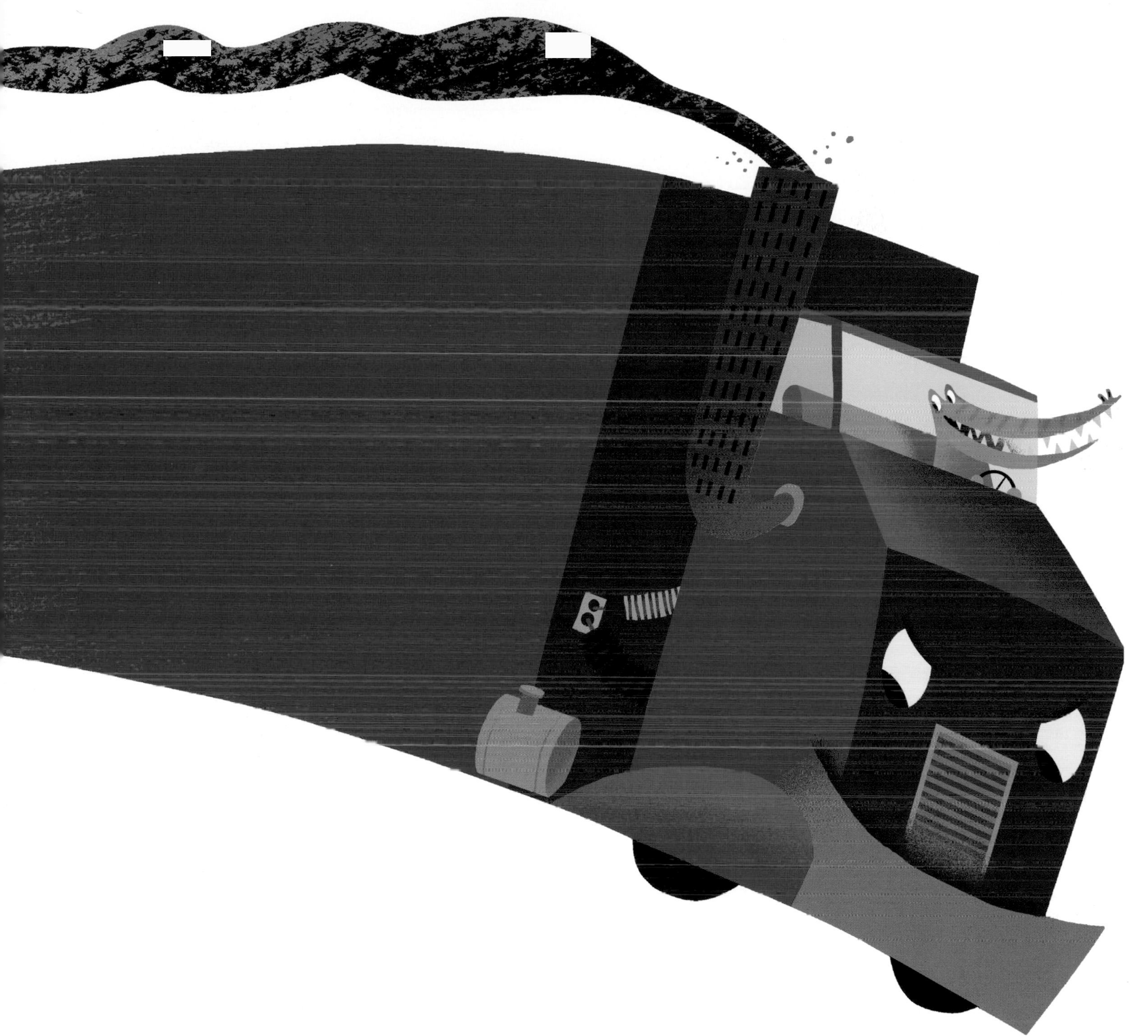

High-tech NEW truck—
go, go, GO!
Creaky OLD truck
go . . . so . . . slow.

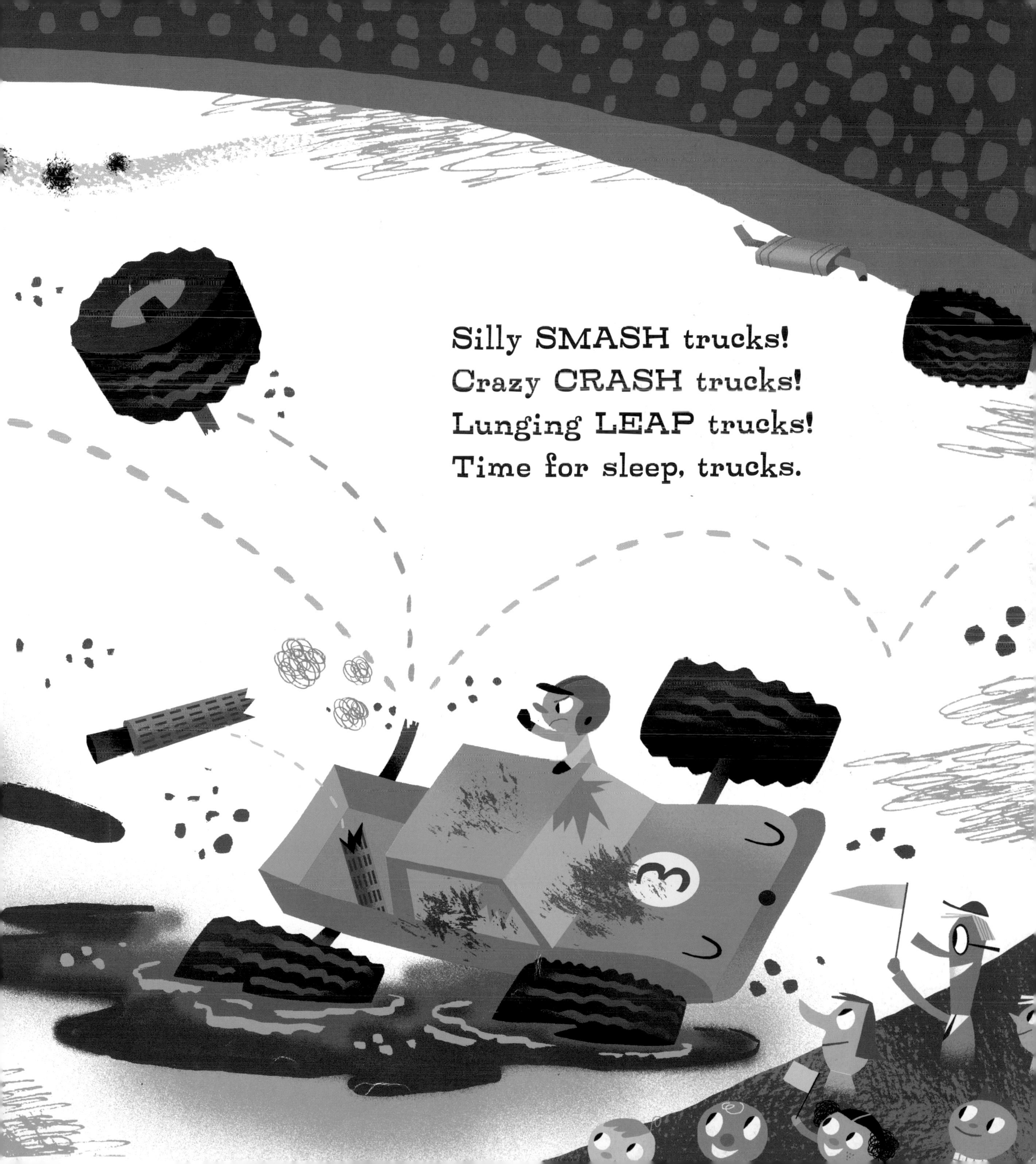

Silly SMASH trucks!
Crazy CRASH trucks!
Lunging LEAP trucks!
Time for sleep, trucks.

A SEA-LIFE truck—
what fishy fun!
Look out below—
you might CATCH one!

Trucks with cakes
and big balloons!
Party trucks play
party tunes!

Daring brave truck!
In-a-cave truck!
Creaky-bridge truck.
On-a-ridge truck.

Trucks bring presents—
you're in luck!
Pull the handle . . .
THANK YOU, TRUCK!

Trucks will work
till work is done.
Trucks are COOL—
they're number one!

A truck
for YOU?
Hey, sounds
like FUN!
HONK HONK
HONK HONK
HONKKA HONKKA

For Gabriel and Elias —
my backseat drivers who moved up front
P. S.

To Oscar Glenn March, inventor of the mud flap
B. S.

First edition 2017

Library of Congress Catalog Card Number pending
ISBN 978-0-7636-8978-0

17 18 19 20 21 22 LEO 10 9 8 7 6 5 4 3 2 1

Printed in Heshan, Guangdong, China

This book was typeset in Zalderdash.
The illustrations were created digitally.

Candlewick Press
99 Dover Street
Somerville, Massachusetts 02144

visit us at www.candlewick.com